MIGHTY MORPHIN
POWER
RANGERS™
2

READY FOR ACTION!

BATTLE BIKES

The Power Rangers™ are ready to take on Rita and her monster squad with help from their Dinozords™. Every Power Ranger has a Dinozord, each with different moves and skills. These skills combined make

RITA^{TM} ATTACKS!

Lead by Rita Repulsa, the enemy crew that the Power Rangers™ have to face are mean and nasty. Each of them have special powers that make it even harder for the Power Rangers. Rita and her crew make their nasty assault plans in their fortress on the dark side of the moon.

GOLDAR™ Goldar is a winged warrior and is Rita Repulsa's personal bodyguard and chief warrior. He is second in command.

SQUATT™ Squatt is a very strange being. He is half wart hog, half blue berry and does not have much for a brain.

BABOO™ Baboo is a hyperactive alien that does not do much other then whimper. He is constantly whining and kissing up to Rita Repulsa.

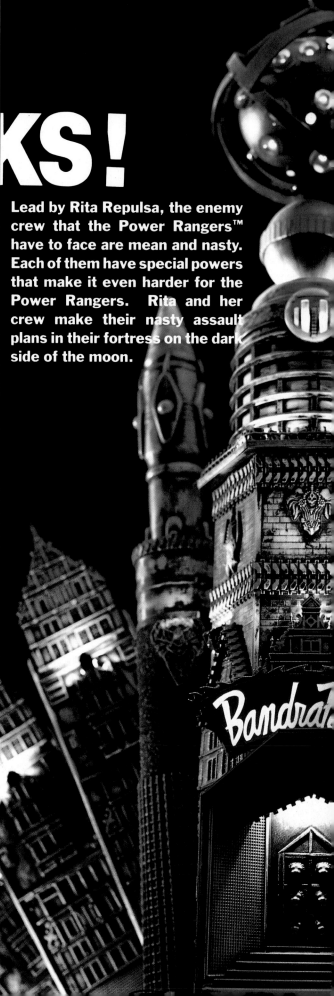

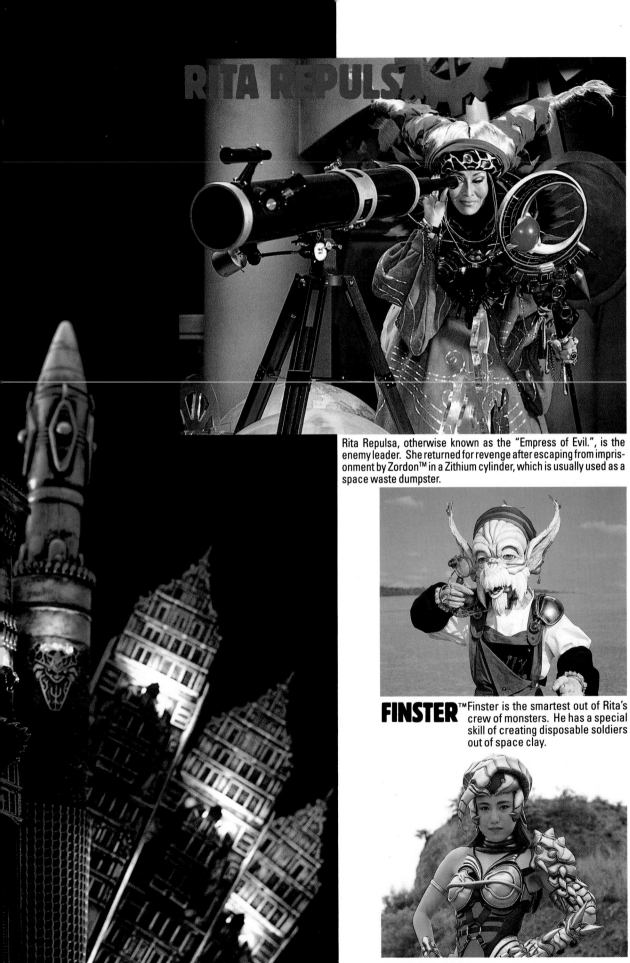

RITA REPULSA

Rita Repulsa, otherwise known as the "Empress of Evil.", is the enemy leader. She returned for revenge after escaping from imprisonment by Zordon™ in a Zithium cylinder, which is usually used as a space waste dumpster.

FINSTER™ Finster is the smartest out of Rita's crew of monsters. He has a special skill of creating disposable soldiers out of space clay.

SCORPINA™ Scorpina is a deadly monster. The long tail and scissors are its weapons.

THE BATTLING ZORDS™!

Jason is the Red Ranger™ and his Dinozord™ is the Tyrannosaurus Rex. Using its claws, it can grab things with incredible strength. The enormous tail can also act as a powerful whip.

The Tyrannosaurus Dinozord™ is piloted by the Red Ranger.

The Tyrannosaurus Dinozord's kick can knock anything down.

THE
MONSTER
SQUAD

The nasty monsters that Rita creates come in all shapes and sizes. As with Rita's crew, they all have special powers that makes life hard for the Power Rangers™. Though they all look different, they have one thing in common, they are… BAD!

COMBINE TO MAKE
MEGAZO

TANK MODE

The Dinozors™ can transform and combine to make a more powerful robot, the Dinotanker™. The Dinotanker is armed with cannons for arms and is also capable of shooting a laser beam from its eyes.

RD™!

ROBOT MODE

When caught up in a little trouble, the Dinozords can combine to make the Megazord. Each of the Dinozords transforms to become a vital part of the Megazord. Now the Power Rangers™ are ready to take on any of Rita's monsters!

DRAGONZORD™!
FIGHTING MODE

The Dragonzord belongs to Tommy, the Green Ranger™. Tommy calls upon his powerful robot using a special flute. With the help of this new friend, the Power Rangers™ are in full force!

MEGA DRAGONZORD™

The Dragonzord is also capable of combining with the other Dinozords™ to create the Mega Dragonzord. With the extra help that the Green Ranger and the Dragonzord will bring to the crew, the Mega Dragonzord is stronger than ever! Watch out Rita!!

NEW TO THE CREW WHITE RANGER™!

The enemy forces take Tommy's power away as Green Ranger™ and leave him helpless. Without his powers, Tommy never stands a chance against the monsters. Zordon™ comes to the rescue and returns Tommy's powers as the White Ranger! Tommy makes a comeback with new weapons and moves.

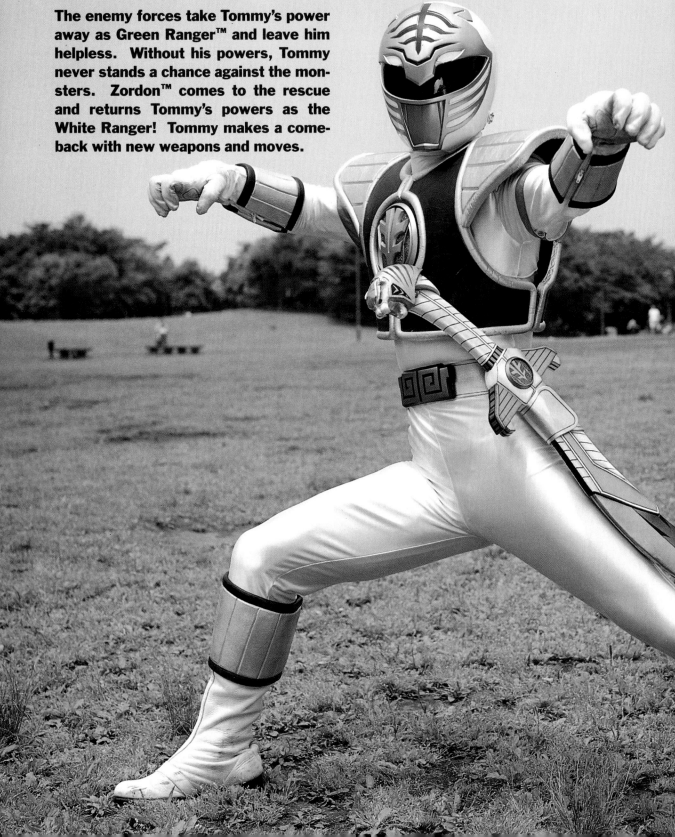

The White Tigerzord™ is able to transform into warrior mode.

TIGER SWORD™

●WHITE RANGER

Tommy, the White Ranger now draws his power from the White Tiger. The armor on his chest is made from a special alloy and can withstand any attack. His new weapon is the Tigersword and he now commands the White Tigerzord™.

MIGHTY MORPHIN POWER RANGERS

Do not fear, the White Ranger™ is here!! With White Ranger on their side, the Power Rangers are charged-up!!